The Person's Angels

FIRST EDITION

ISBN-10: 0692742913
ISBN-13: 978-0692742914 (Gary Drury Publishing)

DrurysPublishing.com

Kentucky

Produced in The United States of America.

Contents

Poems

SILENT TWILIGHT

I miss the call of the whip-poor-will
That echoed through the wood,
And lament the barren stumps
Where majestic trees once stood.

Hush too, the mystic shadow bird
Who hooted away the night,
Then retreated to his vanished den
Before dawn's glowing tight.

The symphonies of twilight time
Were solace to the soul —
Wise men know to leave untouched
What's best in God's control.

How sad the loss of that we love;
Too late we fail to see —
The treasures of the moment
Someday may cease to be.

— © C. David Hay

STARSHINE

Your touch is always present
 Like the wind upon my face.
I listen for your laughter,
I long for your embrace.

All my dreams are given wings,
My mind is free from fear,
The days are full of happiness
Because your love is near.

You light my path on darkest nights,
You show me that you care,
My courage has no limits
As long as you are there.

Somewhere it's written in the stars,
I feel it in my heart;
We are meant to share our lives
And never be apart.

I put no faith in chance or fate
But seek the higher view;
I believe there is a God —
Because He gave me you.

— © C. David Hay

A GRAIN OF SAND

Who am I that GOD should hear
The prayers I utter through the year?
I am but a grain of sand,
But still a part of what HE,S planned.
HE counts each grain and knows that we
Together, make a mighty sea
Of people, who revere HIS ways
And raise our voices filled with praise,
For who HE is and what HE'S done.
For love so great HE gave HIS son,
That we may all receive the choice
To walk with HIM, and hear HIS voice.

— © **Betty Lou Hebert**

A PRECIOUS DAY

The ancient hills in beauty stand
Above this vast and lonely land,
Against a sky of flawless blue,
A soaring eagle scans the view.
The sign of man, a dusty trail,
Winding through the sage and shale.
No sound of man assaults the air.
Only silence everywhere.
Down from the heights on a wintry day,
The frost god flings his jewels away.
Diamonds, lying on the snow,
In icy splendor, beauty show.
Up from the desert, flushed with light,
A thousand wings flash, silver bright,
As small birds rise in disarray,
To greet another precious day!

— © **Betty Lou Hebert**

SEVEN DAYS OF NEVER

Will there ever be
seven days of never
having war, or crime
or corruption in
the arena we call life?
Will there ever be
seven days of never
knowing heartache
through sins and
mistakes we make?
Will there ever be
seven days of never
being lonely due to
circumstance we face?
The world was created
in seven days so the
Bible says, can we
duplicate that phase
so Eden may return?
Will there ever be
seven days of never
saying seven days
of anything anymore?
I'm going to pray for
seven days and whatever
will be, will be!

— © **Gerald Heyder**

FINDING SELF

Standing at front gate to Heaven or Hell,
Though purgatory it may be
I'll rip away the masquerade,
Shed my skin of the world,
Bare my soul to nature's will
Only God and the Heaven's
Will ever know what awaits thee.
When I eject from the belly of this trek
I will be born anew with fresh eyes
Redeemed in this sanctuary
Whether different or same
Time will surely tell the tale
The revelation is for me to discover
Others will chime their voices in the end.

— © **Gary Drury**

OH, MOTHER-EARTH, I AM YOURS OFFSPRING

Oh, mother-earth, I am yours offspring,
I am your loving humbled son,
I spent all my life wandering,
To find new wonders, one-by-one!
My mother-earth, I sing of thee
In thanks for bread and mirthful wine,
How fragrant are fruits on your tree,?
They are delicious, divine!
I'm fond of your animals and birds,
Yours mountains, plains and sparkling seas,
I cannot find the proper words,
In abundant praise let me bend my knees…

**— © Adolf P. Shvedchikov, PhD, LittD
International Poet of Merit**

THE MUSE IS MY ETERNAL LIFE

The Muse is my eternal life,
She is my love, my hope, my fire,
She is my comfort, my desire,
She carries me away from deadly strife.
Sweet Muse, how I love you,
You are my best, devoted friend,
Only to you I wish to send
An amorous sigh and my last adieu!

**— © Adolf P. Shvedchikov, PhD, LittD
International Poet of Merit**

POOR POETRY

Poetry, the queen of human emotions,
Where is your former glory?
Today is another love story,
We are slaves of other potions.
Where is an invisible breath, that aura,
Which feeds your soul and your desire,
Where is that forgotten fire
Of a dance's Muse Terpsichore?
We became the victims of pop-culture,
The poor poetry asks for alms,
Extending her pale trembling arms
Under the threat of a rapacious vulture!

**— © Adolf P. Shvedchikov, PhD, LittD
International Poet of Merit**

RESTLESS THOUGHT

My restless provoking thought,
You are wandering among contrasts,
You are in doubt, you never trust
You suffer when everything comes to naught.
Sometimes you tell to yourself: you ought
To reconsider everything, to revise,
At times you make an unexpected surprise,
Smiling, you comment: it is finely wrought!
And when you causally are suddenly caught,
Be a carefully disguised treacherous trap,
You try insistently to find a gap,
So you will be a winner, my masterful thought!

**— © Adolf P. Shvedchikov, PhD, LittD
International Poet of Merit**

SPARKLE OF JOY

She keeps looking at her ring,
thinking of how wonderful tonight had been,
ecstatic he had finally asked her
to be his wife and share a life with him.

Looking at the ring, she marvels at its beauty
and the deep sense of happiness she feels
being loved by her wonderful man
who fulfilled her wildest dreams tonight.

She dances around her room
holding his picture close to her heart
then kisses the image of her loving man
before she finally goes to sleep.

She sleeps well and dreams about the future
picturing how beautiful life will be
when they take each other in marriage
and finally fall asleep in each others arms.

The sparkle of joy in her eyes
are as brilliant as the shiny stone
and broadcast to the world
how she is loved by him.

— © **Sheila B Roark**

MY MUSE APPEARS

After hiding for many weeks
buried in the deepest recesses of my mind,
my muse has finally surfaced
ready to help me write again.

With its help, my ideas flow
dancing across the waiting paper
with speed and agility
as they form poetic works of rhyming art.

My heart fills with joy and wonder
as I watch the words appear
filling the paper with my thoughts
letting me open my heart to the world.

When the dance of words is completed
I give thanks to the muse within me
realizing it is the vital force
that keeps my writing growing and alive.

— © **Sheila B Roark**

AS I WALK

Softly zephyrs sing to me
on this warm, sunny day
surrounding me with peaceful hope
as I go on my way.

Then I hear the rustling leaves
as soft as velveteen
dance with joy and happiness
dressed in their robes of green

A nearby brook joins in the fun
and babbles out in glee
merrily going on its way
with joyful energy.

And after walking through the woods
I sit and rest a while
enjoying nature's precious gifts
that always makes me smile.

— © **Sheila B Roark**

OLD WOMAN-II

Her face wore many wrinkles
mapping out the woe
she fought against so valiantly,
wherever she would go.

Her hair was limp and thinning
and colored silver gray,
framing her small, wizened face
in such a random way.

Once she walked with power
as she roamed the city street,
but now she stumbles slowly
on sore and swollen feet.

But even though she had grown old
since life had drained her dry,
I still saw youthful beauty
in the twinkle of her eye.

— © Sheila B Roark

POP'S HONEY-FRIED CHICKEN

the golden crunch hangs
crisp in the October
evening over

the Alvarado, Texas roadside stand

brings back
every Sunday dinner at
Aunt Credith's farm outside Frankfort, Kansas

steamy mashed potatoes
melting her hand-churned butter
homemade biscuits
field corn
sliced tomatoes
Guernsey milk
chocolate cake
and chicken

mounds
and mounds
of Leghorn chicken

golden
fried

— © **Sheryl L Nelms**

GRANDMA'S HELPER

chubby hands help
roll out sugar
cookie dough

short stabs
with a circle cutter
shape them

tiny fingers
scrape up
fresh
cut

cookies

pat them into patched blobs
circling the black baking sheet

tongue licks
globbed dough
from impatient lips

toes tap
with the timer
until the cookies

are baked

and cool enough to pop
into a waiting

mouth

— © Sheryl L Nelms

SINAI TRACTOR PULL

my legs
prickle and itch

from sitting
in cheat grass

a toddler
on a blanket

across the road

is eating
iced watermelon

with her hands

dripping
pink juice

from the elbows

— © **Sheryl L Nelms**

SUN DOG

high cirrus
clouds

spangled with floating
ice crystals

refract
a mock sun

fan
iridescence

across
blue

sky

— © Sheryl L Nelms

SAND HILL CRANE

hunkered
deep

in a West Texas bar ditch

one foot
tucked
up

under his wing

the other
plunked

in
iced

water

he
waits

for spring
thaw

— © **Sheryl L Nelms**

"IF ONLY"

We all have the desire for "the good life"
We desire things, we think are necessary
We complain," if only I had more money
"If only I could be thinner"
If I had long beautiful hair
"if only" during my vacation to another
Country I found a painting, worth thousands
Of dollars, and I paid twenty dollars would
I suddenly acquire happiness?
"If only" I married a man that held me
In his heart, instead of beating me on a
Daily basis
How many times while viewing magazines that
Feature outlandish, over the top homes and
Dream "Wow" if only I could afford such luxury
Good fortune and everlasting joy, may seem
Inviting, but life is so breakable
Nobody escapes, there is always twists and
Turns, what can be the explanation?
For cruelty, to other humans suffering
Terminal illness, severe disabilities, finding
Joy in peoples' woes
Some of society are able to accept the "cards
They were dealt"
Perhaps faith plays a large
Role in one's character and ability to offer
A genuine helping hand, be in harmony, with our fellow humans
Wanting the good life isn't a crime, take a moment
To savor the blessings

— © **Sandra Glassman**

MY LYRE

Who does still needs us,
The grains of sand?
Only you, to whom I trust,
My Lyre, without end.
With you I wander
All my life.
Only you work wonders,
With you I'm still alive.
With you I'm ready
To meet new dawn.
With you, my First Lady,
I am not alone.
Sunset is here,
It brings dark night...
Thank you, my Lyre,
Enchanting, bright!

**— © Adolf P. Shvedchikov, PhD, LittD
International Poet of Merit**

MY REDEMPTION IS RELIABLE RHYME

Sweet flowers of lovely spring,
How short is your fragrant day.
I try to gasp time's wing,
But it is slipping forever away.
Who am I, eternity dust,
Tiny morsel of God's clay?
I don't know the answer, alas!
But I cannot bring back this May!
How I hate the prison of time,
I don't want to have right to die...
My redemption is reliable rhyme
Which helps me to survive and to fly!

**— © Adolf P. Shvedchikov, PhD, LittD
International Poet of Merit**

THE PEACEFUL DAY

Nothing is so nice and splendid as spring.
White snowdrop's birth, the first swallow's wing,
The echoing forest is gorgeous and green,
A scene filled with silence, so peaceful, serene,
But sparrows are chirping: spring, early spring...
The water of brook runs quiet downstream,
Be happy, my love, unforgettable dream!

**— © Adolf P. Shvedchikov, PhD, LittD
International Poet of Merit**

MIAMI BEACH

I remember spring's early morning,
Breath of the ocean and humid sand.
The clouds are ruptured, foamy waves are moaning,
Is that the Beginning, the Present, the End?
Monotonous song is humming,
It hits my ear like a knife,
Perhaps it sounded here there was no Miami,
In complete indifference to our death and life...

— © Adolf P. Shvedchikov, PhD, LittD
International Poet of Merit

TUMBLEWEED

Tumbleweed, prickly ball,
Why are you tumbling, why?
Are you looking for the wall
Under the wind-swept sky?
Are you looking for the rest
After a long run?
Are you ready to build the nest
Under the scorching sun?
But wind still blows and blows
Endlessly, day after day,
Where prickly ball goes
Tumbling away...

— © Adolf P. Shvedchikov, PhD, LittD
International Poet of Merit

LAUGHING STOCK

pink plaid slacks
three sizes
too big

hang
from her

bag low
and wet

like a filled diaper

as she
unfolds

from her lamppost perch

like a blue heron
about to take
flight

her eyes dart
nervous

as silver minnows

then she boards
the bus

and is
gone

— © Sheryl L Nelms

ROSA

tap
shuffle
tapping
two gnarled canes
make her way
down
off the brick curb
toward Mesilla Square
stopped at a street sign
she leans into the silver post
ninety-five years old
bent double
she is collage of crusted scraps
basted together
a wad of grey
hair bulges
out of her red scarf
her yellow blouse tucks into the
bloom of green skirt
over blue socks
holed
at the heels
from the loose
flop of feet
toeing their way
into disintegrated moccasins
dangling at different angles
one clawed hand
does a slow
wave
at each low rider
cruising through the corner
so cool
no one sees
her
— © **Sheryl L Nelms**

J. C.

his head flat

on the left side
grows blond hair in
a circling snarl

brown eyes
are clear
and comprehending

at fourteen
he rides
his wheelchair
with finesse
maneuvers tight
corners with flair

his first twelve years
were spent in bed
on his back
head turned
left
looking
down ward hall #5
at Lacy State Hospital

held by
a spastic body
and silver bed
cage
until a new
social worker
started poking whys
through the bars

— © **Sheryl L Nelms**

SUNSHINE

twenty-two years old
black
and beautiful

face always smiling

sparkling
 brown eyes say
he's in there
with soul

even though
the mouth
can't talk
and the diapered
body is nothing
but a breathing skeleton
curled tight

in a frozen fetal twist

the nurses
call him

Sunshine

— © **Sheryl L Nelms**

EDWIN A. NELMS

the quick flick of a smile
is still there

the curly hair still
coal black at 67

the luminous brown
eyes softer now
mellowed
by the Valium

and the body
like a wool sweater
washed in hot water

shrunk
from six foot two
down to five foot four

bones poke out
under his skin

his shriveled bottom
hangs in his slacks
like a limp
beanbag

brittle bone
cancer

has turned him
into a crisp cicada shell
ready to crunch
if I hug him

— © **Sheryl L Nelms**

RUBY JEWEL

As I sit enjoying nature
I see a Cardinal land
and marvel at his ruby coat
so royal and so grand.

I listen to his joyous song
as he sits on the tree
a song that floats upon the breeze,
with heartfelt energy.

He looks just like a ruby
as he sits upon the tree,
singing out in dulcet tones
all day for you and me.

He's brilliant like a gemstone
with a crown upon his head,
a special gift from God above,
a bird that's colored red.

— © **Sheila B Roark**

A BEAUTIFUL TIME

The verdant leaves of blossomed trees
stretch out to reach the rays
that shine down from the azure sky
on sunny, warm spring days.

All the trees invite the birds
to sit on them a while,
and sing their songs of dulcet tones
that always make us smile.

The trees sing too this sunny day
rustling on the air
bringing peace and happiness
to people everywhere.

Squirrels play games upon the grass
then run around the trees,
and butterflies flit here and there
while riding on the breeze.

It is a time of happiness
of wonder and rebirth,
a time that nature comes alive
and fills our hearts with mirth.

— © **Sheila B Roark**

MAGICAL LAND

In the land of magic
where all our dreams come true,
our wishes sparkle like bright gems
up in the sky of blue.

The walkways made of crystal
glow brightly in the sun,
and flowers dance upon the breeze
until the day is done.

This is the land for everyone
who hold on to their dreams,
and live a life of happiness
lit by the bright moonbeams.

Everyone is welcomed here
in this enchanted land,
a place to dream as children do
so peaceful and so grand.

— © **Sheila B Roark**

HE FEELS LOST

He's lost the dreams he used to have
since his world went away,
replaced by such a cold, dark place
filled up with sad dismay.

He's lost the hope he used to have
that made his heart feel gay,
helping him get through his life
as he went on his way.

But what really hurts his tender heart
and makes him cry big tears,
is losing his one special love,
his wife of many years.

He is now an empty shell
who wanders aimlessly,
thinking of his awful loss
he cries in misery.

— © **Sheila B Roark**

MOUNTAINEER

My rugged boots still remain
over bleached bones sans skin
where I took my final walk
along the crystalline stream
until encased into an icy ravine

Along a remote serenity
where bountiful nature and I often
talked. A wilderness man—
I died as I lived—devoted
to earth's cause ultimately
embraced by the deep caverns
of all that I loved and lost.

— © **Diana Kwiatkowski Rubin**

Stories

THE LADDER TO THE ATTIC GOES TO THE STORAGE ROOM OF TREASURES AND MEMORIES

— © Juliet Rhodes Lynch

The winding road, in the back countryside gave one a perspective of farm and country, and ancient back in time houses. There are abandon old homes that are eerie looking, with windows that sag and even broken. There are houses and old barns that have partially fallen into themselves. The old houses speak to those who can hear the echoed voices of the past. The very wood that these houses are built of was at one time, self-cut from an on the property saw mill. The farm land had crafted buildings for food storage from gardens. The Cold Cellar, and Meat Barns, which are for the keeping of Milk, Eggs, Butter, Bacon and the Preserved animals killed on the property. The falling arches of times well warn stairways, and the depth of what and how these people lived, comes back to our mind, and memories.

The old house is sitting up on a mound of dirt, which spreads across a yard, to a fence that goes all the way around the property.

It is a three story house. The Gables, with rounded glass in them, and there are wooden shutters all on the outside windows. One window sits in the center of the very top of the third story. If you look closely you might see what looks like a woman in a wedding dress and her vail.

The inside of the house has a unique appearance of wealth, but also a lot of nick-knacks, an old ornate cherry wood piano, with real ivory keys. A large stone fire place that at one point in time was used to cook upon and kept a good part of the first floor of the rambling old house warm. The upstairs a very slender narrow stairway, to the second floor, that opened into a wide area which led to eight doors. These doors led into eight large bedrooms. Each bedroom had its own stone fireplace and wash stand, and bookshelves. The bathroom was off to the side of the room with oval shaped metal tub and a cosmetics stand. A silver handled hair brush and mirror and comb set lay beside the wash stand.

The hallway was wide and had Chester drawers lining the walls. There was a thin hallway that went toward the back of the house and had two small rooms, one on each side of the narrow hallway. At the very back of this narrow hallway was a lower downed door, from the ceiling with a rope hanging down from the door. What does the door lead to and what are the doors for, that are in the hallway.

It is very exhilarating to have a thoughtful understanding of the two rooms with doors at the end of the narrow hallway. They are Nanny and baby rooms, for the family baby care. The door in the ceiling of the hallway is the pull down stairs to the ATTIC.

THE ATTIC: a remarkable journey in to the forever land of memories.

The rope is an old hangmen's noose, that was used at an old western movie theater lot, for the hanging of criminals in the movies. The stairs make a creaking sound as they are pulled down to allow the beauty of the Attic, to be shown to the memory observers.

The ATTIC: at the top of the stairs is a fantasy land of beauty. The first thing your eyes fall upon is the window in the center of the room that we could see from the outside of the house. The details of this window because it was so far up at the three story house top, and massive Oak tree limbs kept one from viewing its splendor, the window was a of stain glass. Inside the ATTIC room door, the window sparkled, with an array of colors, that made this room filled with prism rainbow colors. A beauty to behold, as one moved forward into the room , there was the wedding dress in Ivory and beads and sparkling diamond like glittering stones. It was on a manikin with a head and wig that looked human. The dress was an antique that belonged to Dolly Madison's daughter and was never worn. Sophenia, died of malaria during the Civil War and was buried in the far meadow of this house, with others from the Civil War, as well as family members. There was next to the dress, a black top Hat that belonged to the man she would never get to marry. Robert Engleman III. He was a well-known Lawyer and Public Defender of his time. In the far corner of the attic sat a large Cherry chest with fourteen drawers of different sizes. There was a small trunk like looking case of wood and intricate painting on it. Expensive Jewelry, that seemed to cascade from some of the drawers. Next to the Cherry chest was a Gramophone, (~ a phonograph the first device for recording and replaying sound.)

The floor of the attic had hardwood that was cut from the popular trees upon the land and refined into boards that were stained and polished. These boards on the floor look perfectly new. There on the other side of the room sat a beautifully carved antique rocker, with a calico pillow of pastel blue material. The rocker was often brought down from the attic when a new baby had arrived in the back room of the house. Nanny Westover, a plump short lady with a rustling petticoat, and the whispering behind the door, and a trifle of a smell of lamp smoke, as she made her rounds, to check out the babies in the two rooms at the back of the house. Along with the rocking chair, there was a beautiful bassinet of White Lace and blue bows. There was another bassinet with pink lace and pink bows.

Laying on an old antique sideboard, (for pies, cakes and cookies and meals prepared for dinners of the refined company, that often

49

came to the house for parties,) was the Civil War rifles and guns that had been found on the property with the soldiers left behind buried out back on the property in the field.

I could feel the spirits of the soldiers as I glanced at the room and felt the crying well within, the room of the sweet babies who once lived in this house. I could see the bride and her Finance' as a betrothed couple and the promise of the forever after, in the here-after.

The doll that was bisque faced, and arms and legs, dressed in a period dress of the Civil War era. The stuffed teddy bear and the clown that was part of traveling circus show. Underneath the ornate pillows for the massive beds- heads leaning against the rafters, was a very old bottle of Bourbon and one of Rum, partially open but not drunk.

Rugs have been rolled up, but the beauty of them can be seen from the unique backing, because of them being Oriental and from the far away, across the oceans black market of years back in another time.

In the drifting and climbing of the ATTIC STAIRS; way back into another time, there is a very delicate fine line of seeing what was, and what History tell us of life before the ATTIC and what memories come from the joy of a visit to the ATTIC.

THE RIDGE IN THE QUIETNESS OF LABOR, AND THE SIMPLICITY OF THE EARTH'S BEAUTY

— © Juliet Rhodes Lynch

The road out the Ridge is a narrow lane with some impassible areas. Lean over edges, having no steel barriers. The Creeks that flow wiggly, on the farm lands edges. They over flow if there is to much rain, or snow run off, with warmer weather.

The stone walls of the mountains are muddy and hang over the rocks, with wild berries, trees, wild flowers. Shrubs, that are hanging from the forest lines into the crevices. The road slithers on in a patch work quilt of gravel, packed down mud, and broken cement chunks and river rock.

There in the wooded area that's cleared away, there in a cut out area is a log house built long ago. Inside is a wood floor from trees of the forest nearby. The stone hearth and fireplace with an old black pot hanging from a metal forged hook. Old flooring with a section or two of smoothed packed mud hardened from years of packing and old fashion Linoleum made from linseed oil, recycled wood , cork dust and limestone and pine rosin.

The windows are glazed glass with small frames, hand - cut and put together by the people who built the log cabin. Tin roof with tin sheets hammered down to protect and keep the occupants dry from the howling winds and rain and winter weather. The old siding on the barns and sheds are the colors of grey, and white and maroon, looking like thin strips of brick and roofing texture.

In the tree line out back of the Cabin are deer grazing and watching new comers on the property, cautiously. This sunny quite crystal clear day, as one sits in the sunlight and shaded tree areas, you can hear the chirping and chattering of the birds, squirrels, wood creatures, discussing the events and sharing the sounds, they have to give to each other of warnings and mate calling.

There in the shadowed grass and patches of sunlight, you can get a quick glimpse of the ''White Winged Butterflies '', Yellow Mini's, and the Monarch, flitting in bunches, as if circling to light on a precious prize of their liking.

In the cleft of the rock base, toward the back of the Cabin is a rock shelf, that looks like an old log road, and horse sled trail, once use for traveling to the mountain cemetery of ''Ancients'', Indians, Mountain Men, Farmers, and Community people, from the country side and hollows of the area.
The flickers of the coming dusk, of twilight that brings reddish, yellow, and rainbow colors across the sky. The deepest Grey lines of colors stream across the sky, giving a quick low darkening gloss to the campfire, built to take away the chill of the evening.

The smell of wild meat cooking, the chickaree coffee, and the wood smoke gives off the delight of memories, of many sustaining campfires of long ago traveler, and homesteaders.

Was this a day of quietness and simplicity and beauty of the earth? Did you feel close to nature, and the spiritual lifting of the Lord.   When, we are filled with the clutter and clamor of the surrounding world and feel frantic, isn't there a place one needs to go to regain the peace and folding arms of quietness? The days are filled with experiences and journey's that we can grasp, and clean out the clutter and clamor and ugly of the world, and put gentle beauty and joy, and nature in its place.

This Road and Ridge is on GABE ROAD, and is the Old Foreman Farm. There is a story that's of many years of living, passed down through the family, and records kept that will and have brought back memories to those who roamed the area, and had relatives and friends who lived there, or came to visit or still live in the area now.

THE YEARS OF LIFE AND MEMORIES

— © Juliet Rhodes Lynch

The life of the people who began to forge and live in this log cabin wasn't an easy life, by any means. It was hard work, and early dawn to dusk labor. The travel was long walking upon the land, and you walked to the Town, of Clendenin, for supplies and seeds (which you sold or traded or bought. Handmade tools, and tools to be bought.) The farm had to be self-sustaining and you raised chickens, and hogs and pigs, cows and a least a dog or two. The often, hunting seasons, brought the deer, squirrel, possum and fowl of the higher ridges, to be preserved and smoked and hung in the barns to keep them for winter meals and family gatherings. There were storage sheds for vegetable, corn, potatoes, hanging of beans (leather britches). Onions and tater's that were older and could be buried in a hole, to bring forth in the early spring. Seed potatoes and onions, they were hidden under ground in the planting cellar, which oft times was used as the cold cellar too. There were storage building and sheds for many parts of life's sustaining items. Even death was handled with the making of the caskets and the burials. Going high up on the mountain to bury their loved ones. Many times in the winter snow, and early spring rains, it was horses and sleds that hollowed a path and the family walked behind, up to the place chosen for burial. The Yellow Popular Lumber was wide board stored in the attic to build the coffins with.

Daylight on Saturday 4:30 A.M. Maw cooked breakfast after Paw built the fire. Pop and boys went to the barn to feed cows and horses. Then, came back to eat breakfast, at 5:30 A.M. Breakfast consisted of Eggs, Fried Apples, Fried Potatoes, Grits and Milk, Biscuits and Pork shoulder meat and good ole churned butter.

Saturday morning after breakfast began with Grist Meal day. Younger boys to go to Grist Mill and men and horses, with bags of shelled corn on the horses' backs. The corn then was ground with. No money changed hands, as Pa was given a measure of 1/10 th of corn. Sold the corn meal to Feed Supply Store in Clendenin, and gave some to family and neighbors. Older boys had to saw fire wood for the coming weeks supply and more for when the bad weather set in.

Lunch was at 12:00 noon and was left over's from breakfast. When meal was over there was always a table cloth put over food.

1:00 P.M. The older boys cut firewood for winter and stacked and stored it, to have enough laid back for the first big storm of coming winter. The young boys coming back from the Grist Mill went to gather the chickens to put in the pen, to be prepared with head chopped off and de-feathered and ready for preparation for Sunday dinner.

5:00 P.M. Supper was leftover. Then Pa cracked nuts, popped popcorn over opened fire, and told stories.

9:00 P.M. Bed time and Pillow Fights upstairs and always the same winners it seems. Slept really good on straw mattress.

Sunday 6:00 A.M. Same as Saturday for breakfast, killed and dressed chicken to cook for lunch, 8:00 A.M. to 5:00 P.M. Day of Rest.

Monday at 6:00 A.M. Walked to Statts store. Then caught the bus at foot of Gabe Hill, to school.

DEPRESSION, COMPRESSION, CONFESSION AND REFRESHION

— © Juliet Rhodes Lynch

Daily Life brings a fight to the finish attitude. If, I can't make this happen, then, I will just put it in the back of my mind and shut it off in my thinking, and our lives in general. WHAT? Why can't we feel our emotions properly anymore? We have become either over sensitive or under-sensitive. It's a fine line between finding our happy spot with life or just turning our head and being miserable. We compress our moments into capsules of layers of " what's next", how long will this last, can I get there on time, whose going to help me, how can I ever get all that done. The second compression is when we are in a relationship and it's either good or bad, and we feel a bit ashamed when things don't seem to be what we thought they might be. We compress are feelings and continue our relationships with friends, family , husband /wife or children. Feelings of emotions, from between miseries, and happiness.

Life, insert's itself into our very being of heart and soul, mind and body. We compress the feeling of trying to figure out what we truly want to do with our lives. We can't make decisions, or we procrastinate and don't do anything about moving forward, in a good or bad direction, in any of life's choices. Depression and Compression mingle together for very unhealthy environment, and not only effect's your life, but dribbles into a flood after it is depressed and then compressed into your mind, body and soul.

So many dark roads of travel and time consuming tasks that makes one so very tired and without mojo to accomplish things. The uplifted mind finds ways to cope and move forward. We can find new directions if we will just learn to look outside the box, of life's blessings and donations, to moving forward. Example; When, some-one dear to us passes away, some people have such grief that they totally become engulfed into themselves, I can't go on without them; I don't know what I will ever do without them. Statements that ''why did God do this to me'', and am I being punished come out of these people's mouths. The grief is so overwhelming that they can't progress in life's daily living of simple basic things. They do not want to live themselves. There is nothing wrong with health grief. We must fix in our minds that if they are Christians and we are also, we have the promise of the LORD himself that we will see and be with them once again in the hereafter. Think of them as being away to complete their existence in a place far better than they were in, and God and them,are preparing a place for us, to never be separated from them ever again. So we must be about preparing ourselves for our own travel to be what God wants us to be, for us to join them. Grief for a season is what helps us to realign ourselves and move forward and complete our earthly tasks.

CONFESSION, IS A WORD THAT WE , CAN'T SEEM TO GET A GRIP on, we fix ourselves upon our own selves and drown, in our pity of how we can never do anything right. We, in our minds are either pious or so awful that we don't know where to begin to confess our inability to accomplish life's journey. Ha, we have heard the old saying ''CONFESSION IS GOD FOR THE SOUL.'' Well, once we confess we give our ugly selves to the Lord and He cleans us up and makes NEW people out of us, and we walk on a NEW journey with our hands clasped tightly in the Lords, Then, what happens?

REFRESHION …. We will walk the dark hills to climb upon the summit to;; ''GOD ON THE MOUNTAIN '' then we will climb every joyous mountain singing the marching songs of ZION… RAISE YOUR VOICES LOUD AND HIGH AND SING HALLE-LUJAH, FOR OUR GOD STILL RAINES AND HE IS ALIVE. AMEN.

Biographies

Born 6/21/41. Parents Eda and William Forcellon. Spouse: Harry W. Barto. Children: William M. Barto. Education: Katherine Gibbs School, Union College, New Jersey, Seton Hall, New Jersey. Extensive travel: Egypt, France, Italy, and England. Occupation: Legal Secretary, Legislative Aide, Writer last 20 years. Memberships: Past President Friends of the Hunterdon Museum of Art, Director of Volunteers at the Hunterdon Museum of Art, New Providence Library Board, New Providence, New Jersey, Raritan Valley College Book Group. Honors: Golden Certificate Awards, Drury Publishing, Plaque of Appreciation from the New Providence Library Board, Listed in Who's Who in America 1999/2000 Who's Who in the East and 2000 Who's Who in America. Have been listed in numerous Who's Who's for all 68 the past years since 2000 including 2007. Personal note: Married for 41 years to husband, Harry, who died in 2001. One son, William, who died in 2000. I love to write. Writing defines who I am.

Publishing Credits: Thirteen stories published by Creative With Words, 2 stories published by Writer's Guidelines and News. One story published in Yesterday's Magazette, One story published in a Reminisce hard cover book "The Fabulous Fifties", 3 stories published in Reminisce Magazine, and two stories published in Good Old Days Magazine. Many stories in Drury anthologies and seven books of stories published by Drury Publishing.

Palm Sunday is a saga about an Italian American family growing up in Brooklyn. The story follows the adventures of this large warm family as they move from Brooklyn to New Jersey and some as far as Florida. However, no matter how far the family is flung from each other they gather each Palm Sunday and Christmas to celebrate the holiday and more importantly the family. The story centers on five female cousins and how they grow and prosper-their loves, joys and sorrows. The story moves between the present time and the past telling of their parents and grandparents and how the family came to this country. The story concerns the grandparents and parents and their lives and fortunes and the children who in turn grow to have children and even grandchildren of their own. Each Palm Sunday and Christmas the family members reconnect and join together sharing their lives.

born and raised in Pittsburgh, PA, lives there still with her husband of fifty-four years, Nick Mother, grandmother and great grandmother, now retired, spends much of her time reading and studying her Bible, working on her writing, which she has been involved in now for nineteen years. She writes poetry and short stories and loves the small press magazines from across the country which give her a chance to have her work published for which she is most grateful Having no formal education other than her GE.D. for a high school diploma, she believes whatever talent she may have has been given to her as a gift from her heavenly Father, to share her feelings which may in some way, be just what someone would like or need to hear. She hopes her writings express her passion for life, her love and devotion to God, family and country. All glory be to the LORD.

I'm widowed and live in the country, in north Idaho, with my handicapped son. We enjoy the life here and all the wildlife we see. I have two older offspring who are married.

I've been writing for many years, actually since I was around ten years old and have been writing steadily for the past fifteen years or so.

My interests are many and varied. I love to travel, read, write, do craft work, garden, cook, and enjoy music of many kinds.

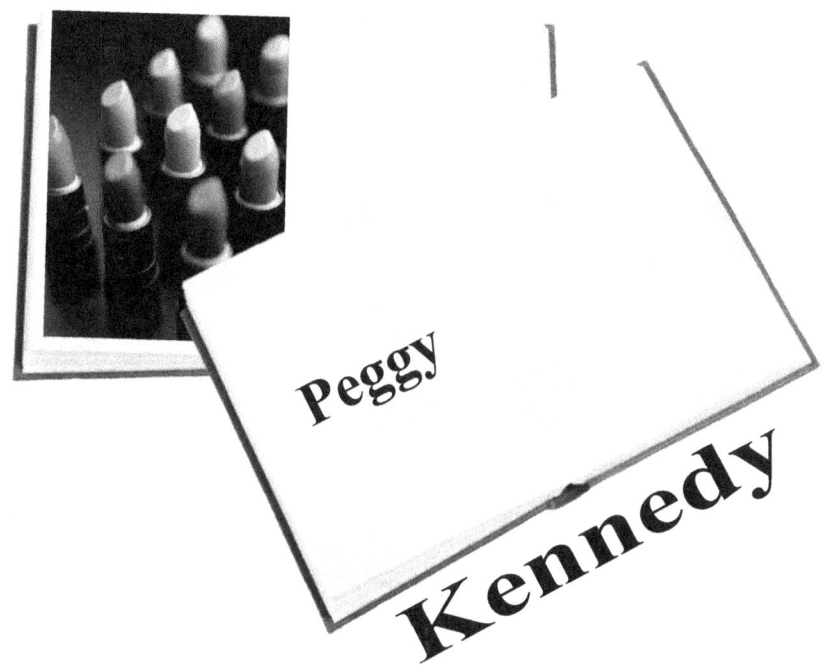

Peggy Kennedy

has published over 600 poems, six stories, one short short story, and one essay. She is currently published in Gary Drury Publishing anthologies and the Drury Gazette and Inside Passages, the last published in Ketchikan, AK. where she currently resides.

She has been published for forty five years. She is currently working on a novel, Wolf's MOON. She practices green daily. She has been listed in WHO'S WHO IN POETRY for fifteen years.

Juliet R. Lynch

Topics for my Poetry and Writings come from inspirational and personal life experiences. 2-Who's Who in Women's Executives 1989, 1990 World of Poetry . . . 2-Who's Who in Women's Executives 1991,1993. World of Poetry. 2 Golden Poet Trophy Awards 1989,1990. 4-Awards of Merit 1987, 1988, 1989, 1990. 2-2000 Noble American Woman 1991, 1992. 1-West Virginia State College Certificate of Merit. 2-American Poetry Association. 4-Awards Trophies for Poetical Achievement, 1989, 1990, 1994, 1996.

The American Poetry Association has printed some of her works in the following Anthology Treasure Books. American Poetry Anthology 1987 and 1990. Best New Poets 1989 and 1990. Loves Greatest Treasures 1988. The World of Poetry has printed some of her Poetry in the following Anthologies. Great Poems of the Western World. World of Poetry 1989 and 1990. World of Poetry 1989 and 1990. World Treasury of Golden Poems. Mrs Lynch has received listings in publications as follows: Anthology listing 2000 NOTABLE AMERICAN WOMEN. Who's Who World Wide Platinum 1992. Professional Societies, The American Biographical Association, The International Platform Association, 25 Year Member of the Charleston Woman's Club, 36 Year Member of the Clendenin Woman's Club, American Biographical Inner Circle, Who's Who World Wide Platinum 1993, West Virginia Writer's Inc., The National Library of Poetry, Golden Rod Conference of Writer's, Clendenin Public Library Board, Clendenin's Writer's Group. Publication by the Author: Joy In The Morning, Book of Written Poetry, Writings and Reading's for Community Affairs, Flames of Mame historical novel Drury's Publications . . . Anthologies and Publications of Poetry and Writings, The Clendenin Herald Newspaper and The Clendenin Town and Country Newspaper, The Country Times Newspaper, Certificate from Gary Drury Publisher Writer Laureate for Juliet Rhodes Lynch.

Sheryl L. Nelms is from Marysville, Kansas. She graduated from South Dakota State University. She has had over 5,000 articles, stories and poems published, including fourteen individual collections of her poems*. She is the fiction/nonfiction editor of The Pen Woman Magazine, the National League of American Pen Women publication, a contributing editor for Time of Singing, A Magazine of Christian Poetry and a three-time Pushcart Prize nominee. *For longer credits listing see Sheryl L. Nelms at www.pw.org/directorv/featured

Adolf P. Shvedchikov

Russian scientist, poet and translator

Born May 11, 1937 in Shakhty, Russia. In 1960 he graduated from Moscow State University, Department of Chemistry. Ph.D. in Chemistry in 1967. Senior researcher at the Institute of Chemical Physics, Russian Academy of Sciences, Moscow. Since 1997 - the chief chemist of the company Pulsatron Technology Corporation, Los Angeles, California, USA. Doctor of Literature World Academy of Arts and Letters.

He published more than 150 scientific papers and about 600 of his poems indifferent International Magazines of poetry in Russia, USA, Brazil, India, China, Korea, Japan, Italy, Malta, Spain, France, Greece, England and Australia. He published also 17 books of poetry. His poems have been translated into Italian, Spanish, Portuguese, Greek, Chinese, Japanese, and Hindi languages.

He is the Member of International Society of Poets, World Congress of Poets, International Association of Writers and Artists, A. L. I. A. S. (Associazione Letteraria Italo-Australiana Scrittori, Melbourne, Australia). Adolf P. Shvedchikov is known also for his translation of English poetry ("150 English Sonnets of XVI-XIX Centuries". Moscow. 1992. "William Shakespeare. Sonnets." Moscow. 1996) as well as translation of many modern poets from Brazil, India, Italy, Greece, USA, England, China and Japan.

In 2013 he was nominated for the Nobel Prize for Literature.

I have lived in Columbus since 1988, and I am an Ohio native. I started writing poetry in 1994. My other hobbies include camping, biking, reading, and photography, to name a few. I have an associate degree in electronics from Columbus State Community College. I currently work for an electrician's shop on the north side of Columbus. We design and build circuit boards from the ground up.

Marian H. Youngquist

was born and raised in Salem, Oregon. Throughout her ninety years she has written for newspapers, magazines and won prizes for plays and poetry. After three novels— *Procula, The Rocky Road Year, A String of Pearls*, and a memoir (private), she is at work on a fourth novel. She also lectures on Roman history. She and her husband Ted, a retired Lutheran minister, live in Wauwatosa, WI. They have four children, six grandchildren, and four great granddaughters.

Born: September 24, 1927, Archer, Florida, lived also, total of 30 years in Kansas City, Kansas; Chattanooga, Tennessee; Louisville, Kentucky, and Detroit, Michigan. It was in Louisville when I began writing songs and poetry around 1977, Basically writing of my life. I have lived every one of them. They are about people who have touched my life in a special way, nature, my pets, love, spiritual. God has been my soul teacher and mentor. Numerous awards. I leave my works to bear witness to Christ Jesus. **Parents:** Zofia and John Gocek. **Spouse:** Charles R. Walden. **Children:** Lisa Maria Walden.

Index

www.druryspublishing.com